Puffin Books
Editor: Kaye Webb
Another Lucky Dip

Charles, the boy with a Useful Bag, is already a firm favourite with everyone who has met him in the first *Lucky Dip* book or heard about him on *Listen with Mother.*

Here he is again in some more beautifully true to life stories, such as the one about the long morning he spends before it is time to go to his friend's party, or how he plays at writing letters in his summer-house office, or goes to the beach with his 'Granny-by-the-Sea'.

Also in this new Lucky Dip is a rich variety of characters including the lonely glass bird on a Christmas tree, a little girl who sees some tiny men walking through the grasses, treasure-hunting for their king, and some delightful mice.

In fact this is a collection to please a child in both his matter of fact and his imaginative moods, and there are few to beat Ruth Ainsworth for storytelling.

Another Lucky Dip

Ruth Ainsworth

Illustrated by
Shirley Hughes

Puffin Books 

Puffin Books, Penguin Books Ltd,
Harmondsworth, Middlesex, England
Penguin Books Australia Ltd, Ringwood,
Victoria, Australia
Penguin Books Canada Ltd,
41 Steelcase Road West,
Markham, Ontario, Canada
Penguin Books (N.Z.) Ltd,
182–190 Wairau Road, Auckland 10,
New Zealand

First published by William Heinemann Ltd
in the *Ruth Ainsworth Book* 1970
Published in Puffin Books 1973
Reprinted 1974, 1976

Made and printed in Great Britain by
Cox & Wyman Ltd, London, Reading and Fakenham
Set in Monotype Bembo

Contents

1. Charles's Long Morning

One day, Charles woke up feeling excited. In the afternoon he was going to a party at the house of his friend Jane. It was Jane's birthday. Charles talked about the party while he was getting up and having his breakfast. He *did* wish it was time to get ready and go!

'What shall I do all the morning?' he asked his mother.

'Why don't you play out in the garden?' she said. 'The sun is shining and there are always lots of things to do outside.'

So Charles went into the garden. First he bounced his ball on the path. It was a brown, rubber ball and it bounced well, but it kept rolling off the path and disappearing under the rhubarb leaves. Then he had to creep under the leaves to find it. So he soon got tired of playing with his ball.

'Is it time for the party?' he asked.

'No,' said his mother. 'It is only nine o'clock.'

Then he got his tricycle out of the shed and rode up and down the lawn. The lawn sloped and he liked riding *down* the slope, ringing his bell. But it was hard work riding *up* the slope. It made his legs ache. So he got tired of playing with his tricycle.

'Is it time for the party?' he asked.

'No,' said his mother, 'it is only ten o'clock.'

Then he put his teddy bear in his wheelbarrow and gave him rides round the house. Round and round and round they went. Sometimes he ran and then the wheelbarrow went bump – bump – bump – and teddy bear fell out. So he soon got tired of playing with his wheelbarrow and went indoors to find his mother.

'Is it time for the party?' he asked.

'No,' said his mother, 'it is only eleven o'clock.'

Charles went back into the garden to the place where the foxgloves grew. They were very tall, taller than he was. Some were white and some were pink. They were nearly over and many of the flowers had dropped off on the ground. Charles managed to find ten white flowers and he fitted them on the tops of his fingers and his two thumbs. They felt cool and soft. Then he crept into the kitchen and said to his mother, 'Shut

your eyes. The Foxglove Man has come to tickle you.' So she shut her eyes and he tickled her face with his white, foxglove fingers and stroked her neck and arms.

'You mustn't laugh, or the Foxglove Man will be angry!'

She tried not to laugh, though the foxglove fingers tickled terribly. Then Charles let her open her eyes and they both laughed and the foxglove fingers fell off.

'Is it time for the party?' he asked.

'No, it is only twelve o'clock,' said his mother. 'Why don't you take your rug and spread it in the shade and lie on it for a little while?'

Charles took his rug and spread it in the shade and lay down on it. The daisies on the lawn looked quite tall when he lay down flat. A little beetle was sitting on one daisy and when the wind blew, the daisy swayed to and fro, to and fro, and gave the little beetle a ride.

A grasshopper was chirping, 'Chip! Chip! Chip!'

A bird in a bush was talking to her babies, 'Chirrup! Chirrup! Chirrup!'

The leaves on the trees were rustling, 'Sh-wish! Sh-wish! Sh-wish!'

Charles felt very sleepy. He closed his eyes. He fell asleep. When he woke, his mother was bending over him.

'Is it time for the party?' he asked.

'It is one o'clock,' she said. 'When you have had your dinner and washed yourself and put on your clean blue suit, it will be time to start.'

Charles jumped up and ran indoors. The party was almost there. The long morning was over.

2. Pepper and Salt

There were once two little kittens who were brothers. They were both born on the same day, so they were twin brothers. They did everything together. When one opened his eyes, the other opened his eyes too. So they *both* opened their eyes.

When one learned to lap milk out of a saucer, the other learned to lap milk out of a saucer too. So they *both* lapped milk out of a saucer.

When one began to chase his tail, the other began to chase his tail too. So they *both* chased their tails.

One kitten was all white. He was called Salt. The other was white with patches of grey fur here and there. He was called Pepper. They had a nice, kind, sleepy mother called Mrs Tabby. They all slept together in a box under the kitchen table.

One day, Salt said to Pepper: 'I can climb higher than you!'

'No, you can't!' said Pepper. '*I* can climb higher than *you*!'

'Let's find a tall tree and I'll show you,' said Salt.

'Yes, let's,' agreed Pepper. 'And *I'll* show *you*.'

They ran into the garden and found a tall fir tree. It went up – up – up – higher than the house. The little kittens began to climb. They had never climbed a tree before and they did not enjoy climbing this one. The

bark was rough and slippery. The green, pointed leaves pricked their soft pink noses. But they went on and on, higher and higher. At last they reached the top.

'We are on the same branch,' said Salt, 'so we are as high as each other.'

'So we are,' said Pepper. 'Now we must go down. Mother will be wondering where we are.'

But they couldn't get down. There was no room to turn round and they dared not climb backwards. They were stuck fast. The ground looked a terrible way off. If they fell, they would certainly break some bones.

A big bird flew over the tree.

'Miaow! Miaow! Miaow!' cried the kittens. 'Please help us to get down.'

But the big bird flew on its way, calling: 'Cuckoo! Cuckoo! Cuckoo!'

Then an aeroplane dived out of the clouds above them.

'Miaow! Miaow! Miaow!' cried the kittens. 'Please help us to get down!'

But the aeroplane went zooming on its way, z-z-z-z-z.

The sun set and the night wind blew through the garden, shaking the fir tree.

'Miaow! Miaow! Miaow!' cried the kittens. 'Please blow us down to the ground.'

But the night wind went whistling on its way, whoo – oo – whoo.

Oh dear, thought the kittens, we shall have to stay here all night. How cold and hungry and miserable we are!

Just then, far below, they saw two small green lights, close together. They were bright and they moved. They stopped at the foot of the tree. Then they began to climb up the tree, higher and higher and higher. What could it be? Then the kittens heard a comforting voice saying, 'It's time you were in bed and asleep.' It was their own mother, Mrs Tabby, and the two green lights were her green eyes, shining in the dark.

First she carried Salt down the tree in her mouth. Then she carried Pepper down the tree in her mouth. The kitchen window was not quite shut and they all squeezed through and snuggled down in their box under the table.

Salt purred and Pepper purred and Mrs Tabby purred and they purred themselves to sleep.

3. Jeremy and his Noah's Ark

One day, a little boy called Jeremy decided he would play with his Noah's Ark. It was kept on a high shelf in the toy cupboard, but he stood on a wooden stool and stretched up, up, till he could just reach it. Then he stepped down from the stool and carried the Noah's Ark very, very carefully to the table.

It was an old Noah's Ark, much, much older than Jeremy who was only four. It had belonged to Jeremy's father when *he* was a little boy. Jeremy's father must have been very careful and gentle as not one of the animals was badly broken. There was a chip off one camel's hump and a black, spotted pig had to stand on three legs instead of four, but that was all. And of course some of the bright paint had faded.

The Noah's Ark was shaped like a boat, with a house inside it. The boat part was green, with wavy lines running round to look like waves of water. The house part was white, with four square windows. The roof was red, with a white dove painted on the top. The roof lifted right off, like the lid of a box, and Jeremy could dive his hand inside and take out the animals.

Jeremy began to take out the animals in pairs, two by two. He stood two yellow lions side by side. Two striped tigers side by side. Then two spotted leopards and two white sheep. Soon there was a long, long line of animals winding across the table.

There were two Noah's Ark people as well as the animals, both with flat, round hats and blue coats. They were Mr and Mrs Noah. It was easy to tell which was which, as Mr Noah had a white beard and carried a stick. Jeremy put Mr Noah at the back, to drive the animals along, and he put Mrs Noah at the front, to lead them in the right way.

But today there seemed to be another person inside the

Ark, as well as Mr and Mrs Noah. Whoever could it be? Jeremy lifted the strange person out and found that it was a small green Elf.

The small green Elf wriggled out of Jeremy's hand and took off his pointed green hat and said:

'Good afternoon, Boy.'

'Good afternoon, Elf,' said Jeremy. 'What are you doing in my Noah's Ark?'

'I was hiding there,' said the small, green Elf. 'I hoped you would soon want to play with the Noah's Ark and then you would find me inside. I've always wanted to have a ride on an elephant, like children do at the zoo. Could I have a ride on one of your elephants, please?'

'Yes, you may,' said Jeremy. 'I'll lift you on to his back and give you a ride up and down the table.'

So he lifted the Elf onto the back of one of the elephants and the Elf sat very straight and still, holding on to the elephant's big grey ears. Jeremy made the elephant walk to the far end of the table and back again. Then he made the elephant run a little and the Elf had to hold on very tightly with both hands.

'That was wonderful!' said the Elf. 'Simply wonderful! May I ride on one of your camels?'

'Yes,' said Jeremy, 'you may.' And he put the small

green Elf on the top of the camel's hump and made the camel walk to the far end of the table and back.

'Make him run, please,' said the Elf, and Jeremy made the camel run and the Elf clung on tightly and laughed as he went bumpety-bump, bumpety-bump.

'Thank you very much for the rides,' said the Elf. 'I must go home now. Good-bye!' He jumped on to the window-sill and climbed down the ivy and disappeared.

Jeremy put his animals back into the Ark, two by two. Two yellow lions. Two striped tigers. Two spotted leopards. Two white sheep and all the others. Then he

saw the Elf's green, pointed hat on the table. He had left it behind by mistake.

'I'll let Mrs Noah have it till the Elf comes back,' thought Jeremy, and he perched the pointed hat on top of Mrs Noah's flat one. It was very smart indeed.

Mrs Noah looked pleased and I am sure she was pleased, too, because ladies usually like to have new hats.

The small green Elf hasn't come back for his hat yet, so Mrs Noah is still wearing it. Do you think he has forgotten all about it? Or perhaps he has another one at home.

4. Charles and Jenny

'Will you come and help me to put up the camp bed in your bedroom, Charles?' said his mother. 'Your cousin Jenny is coming to stay. She is four, like you.'

As they spread the sheets and blankets on the little bed, Charles wondered what Jenny would be like. He had not seen her for so long that he could not remember anything about her.

'You will enjoy having someone to play with,' said Mother.

'Yes,' said Charles, though he did not look pleased.

‘She can play with my toys but she can’t see what is in my USEFUL BAG. That’s a secret.’ His blue bag was slung over one shoulder and he gave it a pat and smiled. Only he knew what was inside.

Jenny came the next day. Charles thought she looked very nice. She had short, yellow braids, tied with red ribbons.

He showed her his toys in the cupboard and on the shelf

and then she caught sight of the blue bag which he had hidden behind the box of building blocks.

'What do you keep in this big bag?' she asked and before Charles could stop her, she had opened the mouth of it and put in her hand.

'Leave my bag alone!' shouted Charles. 'It's my very own secret bag. Give it back!' and he snatched at the bag.

'I only wanted to have a LOOK!' shouted Jenny, holding fast to the string.

Just then Mother came in to say that dinner was ready. Jenny let go of the string and Charles carried the bag into the dining-room and hung it on the back of his chair, while he ate.

After dinner Mother said to them, 'I have an idea for an indoor game. It's too wet to play in the garden. But I need two empty match-boxes, one each. And I can't find two anywhere. It is a pity.'

Charles smiled and opened his blue bag and fumbled about inside and brought out two empty match-boxes.

'What a useful bag!' said Mother. 'There's no guessing what's inside. Now this is the game. See how many tiny things you can collect in your match-box. But you must only have one of each kind. You can go where you like in the house.'

Charles was still a little bit cross. 'Jenny's match-box is bigger than mine,' he grumbled. 'It will hold more things.'

'Let's measure and see,' said Mother. So they laid one match-box on top of the other and they were exactly the same size.

Then Charles and Jenny ran off to look for tiny things to put in their match-boxes. They went everywhere, upstairs and downstairs, in and out of the bedrooms, in and out of the dining-room, in and out of the kitchen. They got out of breath with running and their cheeks were red and hot. Once they bumped into each other in the hall and they both laughed.

'I've found something else,' said Jenny, taking a pin off the pincushion.

'So have I,' said Charles, dropping a tiny glass bead into his match-box.

It would take too long to tell you ALL the things they managed to squeeze in. When Mother called, 'Time is up,' the lids would barely slide on, the boxes were so full. They emptied them out on the kitchen table and Mother counted them. Jenny had twenty-five things and Charles had one less – he had twenty-four.

I will tell you some of Jenny's things: a piece of cotton, a cornflake, a feather, a button, a pin and a crumb.

Now I will tell you some of Charles's things: a match, a bead, a grain of rice, a stamp, a raisin and a hair. The hair was a curly brown one. He had pulled it out of his own head.

Charles was not at all cross now. He did not mind Jenny having one more thing than he had.

'Let's play this game again,' said Charles. 'Can we go out in the garden now the rain has stopped? Would you like to play it again, Jenny?'

'Yes, I would,' said Jenny.

'You can play it in the garden if you wear wellingtons,' said Mother. So they put on their wellingtons and ran outside.

There were not so many tiny things in the garden, but they collected petals and leaves and seeds and berries. When the time was up and Mother counted, Charles had twelve things and Jenny had eleven.

After tea, Charles opened his Useful Bag and told Jenny she could look inside if she wanted. It was half full of things to keep other things in: there were tins and little bottles and match-boxes and jars with screw lids. 'We might play shop with all these good things,' said Jenny.

'So we will, tomorrow,' said Charles. 'We will ask Mother to give us some real rice and coffee and sugar to put in the jars.'

Charles was glad that Jenny had come to stay a while at his house. Jenny was glad too.

5. Crackers the Squirrel

Once upon a time, there was a family of squirrels who lived in a beech tree. There was a father squirrel and a mother squirrel and three little squirrels. They had a very happy life in the beech tree, playing among the branches.

In the autumn, when the beech-nuts were ripe, they ate as many as they wanted and hid the rest in holes at the foot of the tree, to eat later on.

Near the beech tree was a house and the little squirrels, if they crept to the tip of a long, bendy branch, could jump on to one of the window-sills. This window belonged to the nursery. The squirrels pressed their furry, whiskery faces against the glass and looked inside. They saw a family of children eating or playing or listening to the radio.

One of the squirrels was called Crackers because he was good at cracking nuts. He spent hours peeping in the window. He looked at everything in the room, but best of all, he liked the shelf where the toy animals sat. There was a whole row of them: a teddy bear, a panda, a rabbit with velvet ears, a yellow duck and a big white elephant.

He often wished he were a toy squirrel instead of a live one and could sit on the shelf with the other toy animals. It looked so cosy in the room with the bright fire and the warm carpet on the floor and the pictures on the walls – much nicer than being out of doors in the wind and the cold.

One afternoon, Crackers crept along the bendy branch and jumped on to the window-sill. The nursery was very quiet as the children had gone out to tea. The fire was blazing brightly and he could see the shelf of toy animals. The window was open a little way and he squeezed through and sprang on to the floor. He ran across the room – climbed on the back of a chair – and jumped on to the shelf.

There was a space between the teddy bear and the elephant and he sat down in the space, feeling very pleased with himself. But the teddy bear and the elephant did not look very pleased. They frowned and turned their backs on him. Presently the teddy bear growled:

'What shop did you come from?'

'I didn't come from a shop,' said Crackers. 'I came from the beech tree.'

'WE all came from shops,' said the other animals. 'Large, important shops with counters and glass cases and telephones.'

'How much did you cost?' asked the white elephant.

'I don't think I cost anything,' said Crackers.

'WE all cost a lot of money,' said the other animals. 'WE are very expensive indeed.'

'What are you stuffed with?' asked the panda.

'I don't know. I don't think I am stuffed with anything. I'm just squirrel all the way through.'

'WE are all stuffed with the very best stuffing,' said all the other animals.

Crackers hung his head. He was sorry he was such a queer creature with no proper stuffing.

'Do sit still!' grumbled the yellow duck. 'We never fidget on this shelf.'

'Can't you stop sniffing?' complained the rabbit with velvet ears. 'I have such good ears that I can hear ever sniff.'

Crackers tried to sit very still indeed and not to fidget or sniff. He even tried not to breathe, but he had to take a breath in the end. He felt uncomfortable. He had a tickle at the back of his neck and pins-and-needles in one foot.

Just then a black cat came into the room. The other animals took no notice at all. They did not even turn their heads. But Crackers felt cold shivers go up and down his back. His teeth began to chatter and his whiskers trembled. He wished he were in the beech tree with his mother.

'Is it a nice cat?' he whispered to the teddy bear.

'It's just an ordinary cat,' said the teddy bear. 'She never takes any notice of us. Why should she?'

But the cat was behaving in a strange way. She sniffed and stretched her neck and her green eyes searched every corner of the nursery. Then she jumped on to a chair and stared at the shelf of toy animals. She stared straight at Crackers. She smiled and showed her white, pointed teeth. Then she gave a deep, hungry growl – .

The growl was too much for Crackers. He gave a leap off the shelf – on to the table – then on to the window-sill – through the window – and on to the bendy branch. Before you could crack a nut, he was safe in the nest with his mother and father and the other little squirrels.

Crackers never even looked through the nursery window again. He did not want to be a stuffed animal and sit still all the while, and he did not want ever to see the black cat again with her green eyes and white, pointed teeth.

He was very glad he was a live squirrel and lived in a beech tree.

6. Brother Mouse and Sister Mouse

Once upon a time there were two little mice. They were brother and sister and they lived together on the beach in a bathing-hut. This sounds a very odd place for two little mice to live, but they were really quite comfortable. They had a snug hole in a corner, between two boards.

What could they find to eat, living on the beach? Well, they could not eat fishy, salty things like seaweed and shrimps, because mice do not care for fishy, salty tastes. They ate delicious crumbs of cake and biscuits and sandwiches.

Where did they find these delicious crumbs? They were dropped by the children and grown-ups who used the bathing-hut to undress in before they had a swim, and to dress in afterwards. When the children came running and laughing and shivering up from the sea, their mothers nearly always said, 'Here's a nice currant bun, dear, to eat while you are getting dressed.' Or, 'Here is a sandwich – or a biscuit – or a square of chocolate.'

The children always dropped crumbs as they ate and the little mice ran out of their hole, when no one was looking, and gobbled them up. All through the summer the little mice kept fat and contented with their meals of crumbs, but when the summer was over, the children went back to their homes and it was much too cold to go swimming. The man who owned the bathing-hut locked it up for the winter and went away too.

Poor little mice, how cold and hungry they felt. They crept over the pebbles and sand and tried to nibble bits of seaweed, but it was so salty that they had to spit it out. One day, Brother Mouse found half a coconut at the edge of the sea. It was round and brown, rather like a bowl.

'I have an idea,' said Brother Mouse. 'Find me two straight pieces of wood, Sister, about the same size.'

Sister Mouse hunted here and there and found two strong straight sticks. Then Brother Mouse jumped inside the half coconut and took a stick in each paw and said:

'Look, Sister! This is our boat and these are our oars to row with. Jump in beside me and let's go for a sail. We may find somewhere else to live in a place across the sea.'

Sister Mouse was very frightened, but she did not want to be left behind, so she jumped in beside Brother Mouse. Just then a big wave came rushing in, whoosh – whoosh – and in a moment the little round boat was afloat.

Oh, how the boat rolled and tossed, up – up – up – on

one wave. Then down – down – down – on the next. UP – d-o-o-o-w-n! UP – d-o-o-o-w-n! UP – d-o-o-o-w-n!

Sister Mouse began to feel sick but Brother Mouse was too busy with the oars to think of anything else. Soon they got used to being rolled and tossed about and they

began to enjoy themselves. They could see nothing but sky and sea, blue sky above and green waves all round with foamy white tips. They floated on for a very long time and they began to wonder if they ever *would* reach land. Their legs were stiff with sitting still so long and Brother Mouse's arms ached with tugging at the oars.

Suddenly they saw something tall sticking up out of the water.

'Land ahead!' shouted Brother Mouse. 'Land ahead!'

Then the boat bumped into the tall thing and stopped moving.

The tall thing was a huge wooden post. 'Let's climb up the post and stretch our legs,' said Sister Mouse. So they climbed up the post which was slippery with wet, green seaweed and prickly with sharp, pointed shells.

When they were at the top there was a wooden floor to walk on.

'Oh!' sighed Sister Mouse. 'What a lovely smell!'

'Oh!' sighed Brother Mouse, 'I *am* hungry!'

The smell was a mixture of toast and coffee and sausages and plum cake. It came from a large house nearby.

The two little mice crept in through the door, which happened to be open, and found a comfortable home in a hole in a dark corner. They learned that the house was a café at the end of a pier and the wooden post they had climbed up was part of the pier.

The café made a very good home. It was open all the year round, winter and summer, and there was always plenty of food and plenty of crumbs.

Once, someone said to the lady who sold the food: 'I saw a mouse under the table. You must buy a mouse-trap and catch him.' But the lady said: 'Mice? What an idea! Whoever heard of mice living at the end of a pier?'

Brother Mouse and Sister Mouse hugged each other in their safe little corner and felt glad they had left the cold bathing hut on the beach and floated in their coconut boat to this lovely, comfortable place.

7. The Glass Bird

At night, when everyone had gone to bed, the Christmas tree woke up. The dark green branches swayed from side to side, and the little bells rang, and the paper chains rustled. A silver bugle blew 'Toot! Toot! Toot!' and two wooden drum sticks beat 'Tum! Tum! Tum!' on the drum. The Fairy Doll on the topmost bough rose on her toes and turned round and round, waving her wand till the star at the end twinkled like a real star.

There was a glass bird on the Christmas tree. She was very pretty with silver wings and a silver tail. Her feet and her beak were red. She spread her silver wings and flew about the room, pecking at the berries of the holly. Sometimes she rested on the back of a chair or on the

bookcase. She was happy, but she did not sing. There was no other bird to sing to.

Once, when she was flying near the mantelpiece, she perched on the clock and listened to its steady 'Tick-tock! Tick-tock!' There was a mirror hanging over the clock and she saw, in the clear glass, a wonderful sight. It was a pretty little bird with silver wings and a silver tail, and a red beak and red feet.

'Now I shall have a companion,' she said. 'Now I shall have someone to talk to in the long winter evenings.'

She sang, 'Sweet! Sweet!' and the bird in the mirror sang 'Sweet! Sweet!' back again.

She bowed her silver head and spread her silver wings, and the bird in the mirror did the same.

When it was time for the toys to go back to their places on the tree, ready for the next day, the silver bird would not leave the mantelpiece.

'Come back!' rapped the drum. 'Tum-tum-tum!'

'Come back!' blew the bugle. 'Toot! Toot! Toot!'

'Come back!' said the Fairy Doll. 'It is time to take your place.'

'Come back!' said the empty branch. 'Come back and perch on me!' But the glass bird shook her head.

'I shall never come back,' she said. 'I shall stay where I am always, with my new friend.'

When the clock struck twelve, someone in a red coat, with a white beard and a sack of toys on his back, came into the house. 'Oh Santa Claus, do help us!' begged all the toys on the tree. 'The glass bird won't come and perch on her branch. She is looking at herself in the mirror. She thinks her reflection is another bird and she says she will stay there always and never come back.'

'Little bird, come back to your branch,' said Santa Claus gently. 'The tree looks so much better if you are in your place. Come back, little bird.'

'Never! Never! Never!' whistled the glass bird. 'I will never leave my new friend.'

'There is only one thing to do,' said Santa Claus. 'We must get another glass bird and put it on the branch to sit beside her. But how are we to get one? My sack is full to bursting, but there isn't another bird among the things. I have one in my workshop in the Land of Ice and Snow, but that is hundreds of miles away. My reindeer cannot get there and back by morning.'

'I will fetch the glass bird,' said a red aeroplane which was hanging on the tree. 'I can get there and back in no time.'

'Thank you, red aeroplane,' said Santa Claus. 'You will find the glass bird on a shelf just inside the door of my workshop.'

'How shall I find your workshop?' asked the red aeroplane.

'It is covered with holly and mistletoe, and there is a lantern hanging outside,' said Santa Claus, unfastening the string that held the aeroplane to the branch. Then he opened a window. The propellers began to whizz round and the engine began to roar and the pilot, in his helmet and goggles, flew the plane out of the window toward the north.

Santa Claus went back to his sleigh and drove away because he had work to do.

It was nearly morning when the red aeroplane flew back, bringing the glass bird.

'See what I have brought back from the Land of Ice and Snow,' said the pilot, and the glass bird stopped looking at herself in the mirror and turned her head and saw the new bird. She flew to meet him and the two birds bowed their heads and spread their wings and sang a song of welcome.

Then they sat side by side, on the empty branch that was waiting for them.

'Three cheers!' blew the bugle. 'Toot! Toot! Toot!'

'All is well,' said the Fairy Doll, waving her wand.

When the candles were lit on Christmas Day and the

children gathered round to watch and have their presents, they all said:

'How pretty the two glass birds are! They look so friendly, sitting side by side on the same branch.'

8. Charles on a Windy Day

One morning, after breakfast, Charles's mother said to him: 'I should like to wash your Useful Bag today.'

'But it doesn't need washing,' said Charles. 'It's quite clean.'

'Let's look and see,' said Mother, and she spread the bag out on the table. It was very dirty indeed. There were brown marks of mud on it and green marks of wet grass, because Charles took his Useful Bag everywhere with him and he often went in dirty places.

'It is a bit dirty,' agreed Charles; 'but don't wash it today. Not today. Another day.'

'The sun is shining and the wind is blowing,' said his mother, 'and the bag will be dry in a jiffy. Then I will iron it and you can have it back by dinner-time.'

'Y-e-e-s,' said Charles. 'But what shall I do with the things from inside? I need a safe place to put them.'

'You can have this big shopping bag with string handles. That will do just for now.'

'All right,' said Charles, unpacking his things from the blue bag and putting them into the shopping bag. 'But my bag doesn't often need washing. Not again for another year.'

Mother quickly put some soap-flakes in a bowl of water and whisked them up with her hand till the water was all foamy. Then she plunged the bag into the bowl. She squeezed and squeezed till the bag was clean, and after she had rinsed it in a bowl of clear water, she wrung it as dry as she could.

'I'll put it on the clothes line,' said Charles.

'Shall I help as the wind is so strong?' asked Mother.

'Please don't come. Please don't help. I can do it by myself,' said Charles. So he took the wet bag into the garden and got two clothes-pegs from the peg basket in the shed. The line was low and he could reach it. He put a clothes-peg at each corner and watched the wind blow the bag till it was like a blue balloon.

Charles liked to hear the flapping noise it made – flappity – flappity – flap – flap – flap! Then he went indoors to play with his train. When he had played trains long enough, he ran outside to see if his bag was dry.

Oh, what could have happened? The line was still

there, but there was nothing on it. The two clothes-pegs that had held the corners of his bag were lying on the grass.

'Mother!' he called. 'Mother! Come help me! The wind has blown my bag away!'

His mother came hurrying into the garden. She saw the empty line and the two clothes-pegs and Charles's sad face.

'We'll find your bag,' she said. 'It can't be far off. Let's both look. It may be caught in a tree or bush.'

The wind was very strong. It tangled their hair and snatched at the strings of Mother's apron. Up in the sky the big white clouds were scurrying along.

Charles felt sure his bag had gone whirling away, high in the air, so he looked in all the high places. He looked at the tops of the trees and the roof of the house. His neck ached because he bent it back so far. But there was nothing blue caught in the trees or on the roof or by the chimneys.

His mother looked lower down. She searched the bushes and the hedge. But there was nothing blue caught in the bushes or the hedge.

'Perhaps it is miles away,' said Charles. 'Miles and miles away where we shall never find it.'

'Let's walk all round the garden once more,' said Mother. 'Then we can try the garden next door.'

So they walked slowly round the garden, looking among the potatoes and the cabbages and the flowers, searching everywhere. Suddenly Charles cried out:

'Mother! Look! In the long grass behind the summer-house!'

She looked in the long grass and there was the bag. Charles ran to pick it up, but he stopped when he had touched the string.

'There's something *in* my bag,' he whispered. 'I saw it move. A kind of little lump.'

They both watched. There was a small hump at the bottom, not much bigger than a marble.

'It moved. It's alive,' said Charles.

The small hump moved a little way. Then stopped. Moved a little farther. Stopped again.

'Is it a bird?' wondered Charles, 'or a snail?'

The hump moved very quickly, far too quickly for a snail. Charles watched the mouth of the bag. Would the little thing peep out? Did it like being shut up in a bag?

Suddenly a tiny face appeared, the tiniest face Charles had ever seen. It had ears and a sharp nose and bright eyes. And tiny, tiny whiskers.

'A baby mouse!' whispered Charles. 'It has a very lost look.'

The baby mouse came right out of the bag so they could see its little feet and long tail. It looked one way. Then the other. Then it turned all the way around. For the mouse, the grass was a tall forest and it could only peer between the stalks.

'Will it ever find the way home?' asked Charles. 'It's only a baby. Can we have it for a pet?'

But the baby mouse was very sensible though it was so small. It went on looking and sniffing and turning around and trying to remember where it lived. Then it

gave a happy little scamper and darted through the grass and dived into a hole under the summer-house.

'I expect its mother is glad,' said Charles. 'She must take better care of it till it grows bigger.'

Then they went indoors. Mother washed the bag again because it had got dirty and pegged it on the line herself with four clothes-pegs to keep it safe, one at each corner and two in the middle. Charles had a glass of milk and two ginger biscuits.

'Looking for lost things makes me hungry,' said Charles, scrunching his hard biscuits and drinking the last drop of his milk.

9. Mollie under the Apple Tree

One day, a little girl called Mollie was playing in the garden. She was lying in the long grass under the apple tree. It was very quiet, because there was no one to make a noise. She could just hear a bird saying, 'Tweet! Tweet! Tweet!' And a bee saying, 'Buzz! Buzz! Buzz!' And a pony trotting down the lane, Trit-trot! Trit-trot! Trit-trot!

Presently she heard another sound, like very small feet marching along. They went pit-pat, pit-pat, pit-pat. Then, between the tall grasses, came some tiny little men. They were no bigger than Mollie's little finger. Each one carried something to dig with. One had a spade. One had a fork. Another had a trowel. And each carried a sack on his back.

They all had white beards and they looked SO cross and tired. Their faces were red and hot and they grumbled as they walked along.

'I'm SO hot,' said one.

'I'm SO tired,' said another.

'I'm SO cross,' said the next.

'I can't dig any more,' said the one after that, and they all sighed together like this: Sigh! Sigh! Sigh!

'What are you digging for?' asked Mollie.

'We are digging for treasure to give to our King,' said one. 'We want to find pretty things to put in our sacks.'

'Have you found any treasure?' asked Mollie.

'No, we haven't. That's why we're so tired and cross.'

Mollie felt very sorry for them. 'Sit down and rest,' she said. 'It is cool under this apple tree.'

So the little men laid their spades and forks and trowels on the ground. They took off their sacks and sat down. They all took out red spotted handkerchiefs and wiped their hot faces. Then they closed their eyes and had a nice, comfortable doze. While they were resting, Mollie ran indoors and fetched her bead-box. It was full of beads of all kinds, big ones and little ones, coloured ones and plain ones. She found a patch of soft soil and buried some of the beads, not very deeply. She buried the prettiest, the ones that shone like real jewels.

When the little men woke, they yawned and picked up their empty sacks and their spades and forks and trowels.

'Do you know where there is any treasure?' they asked Mollie.

Mollie led them to the patch of soft soil and said, 'Why not try here?'

The little men began to dig and soon one called out, 'I've found some red treasure.' And another called out, 'I've found some blue treasure.' And another called out 'I've found some green treasure.'

They were so happy. They put the shiny beads in their

sacks and when they had finished digging, they said good-bye to Mollie.

'The King will be very pleased with us,' they said. 'He will put all this treasure in a strong, safe box and turn the key. Good-bye! Good-bye!'

They marched off in a line, smiling and chattering. Mollie wondered what the King was like and if he wore a crown, but she never saw him. Perhaps she will, one day, if she is lucky.

10. The Silver Thimble

Have you ever played 'Hunt the Thimble?' I'm sure you have. Everyone goes out of the room except one person who hides a thimble somewhere. Then he shouts, 'Salt fish come to supper!' and everyone comes crowding in from the hall to look for the thimble.

This story is about a game of 'Hunt the Thimble'. A little girl called Sally had a party and the children wanted to play 'Hunt the Thimble'. Sally had the first turn because it was her birthday. When all the boys and girls were outside in the hall, and just Sally left behind, she shut the door and looked round for a good place. It was her own living-room so of course she knew the good places.

Should she put it behind a vase or under a chair? Should she try to reach the top of the bookcase or the TV? In the end she put it on one of the pedals under the piano.

Then Sally opened the door and called out, 'Salt fish come to supper!' and everyone crowded in to search for the thimble. Some looked high. Some looked low. 'Are we warm? Are we getting hot?' they asked. But no one was near the piano so no one was warm. Then, suddenly, Sally cried out, 'The thimble's gone! It's disappeared! It isn't where I put it!'

Her mother looked under the piano and the children looked too and crept about on hands and knees over the floor. But there was no sign of the thimble.

'Oh, Mummy!' said Sally. 'What shall we do? It was your best silver thimble with the tiny lion stamped inside.'

'It must be somewhere,' said her mother. 'Don't let's worry. I'll find another thimble for you to play with instead.'

Now behind the piano was a small, dark mouse-hole and in the small, dark mouse-hole lived a family of mice. The father mouse had seen the silver thimble shining and had darted out, quick as a flash, while Sally was opening the door, and had snatched it up and taken it into his hole. While the children were searching, everywhere, he and his family were admiring the thimble.

'It is made of real silver,' said Father Mouse, biting the edge. 'I shall use it for my own special drinking cup.'

'I think it would make a good plant pot,' said Mother Mouse. 'This is a dark hole and some flowers in a bright pot would cheer it up.'

'It would make me a fine new hat,' said the Girl Mouse. 'I should be proud to wear it.'

'But I want it for myself,' said the Boy Mouse. 'It will make a drum and I shall beat it like this.' He began hitting the thimble with a spoon. It sounded rather tinny.

By this time the mice were very angry with each other. They glared. They glowered. They growled. They lashed their tails and showed their teeth. They were cross all the evening and went to bed without saying good-night to each other, all because of the silver thimble.

In the middle of the night, the mice woke up with a start. A tall, shining person with very long legs was standing outside their hole. 'Snip-snap! Snip-snap!' said the tall, shining person. 'I am the scissors from the work-basket and I have come to get my thimble. Snip-snap! Give me my thimble or I will snip off your whiskers.'

The mice were frightened and shivered and shook, but they did not want to give up their silver thimble.

Then a row of thin, pointed people with scratchy voices stood outside. 'Scratch-scratch! Scratch-scratch!' said the pointed people. 'We are the pins from the work-basket and we have come to get our thimble. Scratch-scratch! Give us our thimble or we will prick you.'

The mice were more frightened and shivered and shook more than ever, but they did not want to give up their silver thimble.

Then a *very* sharp person with a long tail appeared. 'Stitch-stitch! Stitch-stitch!' said the very sharp person. 'I am the needle and thread from the work-basket and I have come to get my thimble. Stitch-stitch! Give me my thimble or I will sew up your hole and you will never be able to get out.'

The mice did not want to be sewed up for ever and ever in their hole so they pushed the silver thimble out of the door and squeaked, 'Take it!'

Then the scissors with shining legs and the pins with sharp points and the needle with a long tail took the thimble back to the work-basket where it belonged. The work-basket had a soft, padded lid, lined with silk, and was a very cosy place indeed, far cosier than a mouse-hole.

Sally's mother was very surprised to find her thimble there the next day. She was surprised, too, to see tiny teeth marks round the edge. But she never guessed they were where Father Mouse had bitten it to find out if it was real silver.

11. Charles Goes to the Office

'Is it all right for me to come over to your garden to play?' asked Pat, the little girl who lived next door to Charles.

'Of course,' said Charles. 'Come through the gap.' So Pat pushed and squeezed her way through the gap in the beech hedge and came into Charles's garden. Charles was walking up and down, swinging his blue, Useful Bag.

'What's in your Useful Bag today?' asked Pat.

'That's a secret,' said Charles. But he added, 'You can feel, if you like, and try to guess.'

Pat began to pinch and poke the bag with her fingers. 'Is that a clothes-peg? It feels hard and wooden.'

'No. That's a thick, thick crayon. It is very special. It writes red one end and blue the other. Feel again.'

'A match-box?'

'Yes,' said Charles. 'It *is* a match-box, but you don't know what's inside.'

'I can feel another match-box,' said Pat, pinching something and shaking it through the bag. 'And soft things like little books. Oh, and hard ones too. Please,

please let me look. I won't tell if it is a secret.'

Charles always told Pat his secrets in the end because she was his friend.

'We'll go into the summer-house and dump everything out on the table,' he said. 'Then you can see for yourself. Come along!'

They ran to the summer-house and Charles turned the bag upside down. Out came a queer collection of oddments, match-boxes and note-books and envelopes.

'They are all important office things,' said Charles. 'Things that men use when they go to the office every day. Here are some clips to clip paper together. Here are lots of little note-books and envelopes. Let's have an office in the summer-house, and do real office work.'

Pat thought it was a good idea. 'I'll get some things from my house,' she said, jumping up. 'I'll be back in a minute.'

She found another pencil and a rubber. Her mother gave her a roll of sticky tape and she looked in the waste-paper basket for some envelopes. She brought her own scissors, too, and a little pot of paste.

Charles and Pat had a lovely morning. They wrote letters in scribble writing because they could not write real writing yet. They put the letters into envelopes and cut out used stamps and pasted them on with Pat's paste. The letters looked *very* important with a whole row of stamps on, instead of just one in the corner.

'We need a pillar-box to drop our letters in,' said Pat. 'Let's look around the garden and try to find one.'

They walked around and around the garden, looking everywhere, but they could not see anything that would do. There was a crack between two stones but some beetles lived there, and they might nibble the letters. Suddenly Charles saw a piece of drainpipe that workmen had left near the shed. It was just right, with a hole at the top to drop the letters in.

Charles and Pat often played at office work after this. Charles's mother found a cork and cut an X on it with her penknife. She let them have just a spot of ink in a saucer and they put the cork in the ink and dabbed it hard on the envelopes. It left an inky circle with a cross in the middle. This made their letters look very important indeed.

One morning, Charles and Pat had been very busy in their office. Charles was writing letters in blue crayon and Pat was writing letters in red crayon. They often clipped several pieces of paper together with a paper clip to make a nice fat letter. Then they stuck some stamps on the envelope and dipped the cork in the inky saucer and banged it on, like this – bang! bang!

'I've just written to the Queen,' said Charles. 'I've asked her if she is quite well and if she wears her crown indoors.'

'I've written to the man at the bank,' said Pat. 'I've said he can send me a sack of money if he wants to.'

'Let's post our letters and then play with our hobby horses,' said Charles. 'We've done enough office work for today. Dobbin and Dapple want a gallop.'

Just as Pat was about to drop her letter into the pillar-box by the shed, a robin flew out and made her jump. 'What is he doing down there?' she asked.

'Let me look,' said Charles and he bent down. At the bottom of the piece of pipe were twigs and leaves and a few feathers.

'He's building a nest.'

'How lovely,' said Pat. 'Of course we can't post any more letters now. Let's hide and see if he comes back.'

They crouched behind the lilac bushes and watched until they saw the father and the mother robin come with bits of twig in their beaks, and then disappear down the pipe. Then the birds flew off for more. Soon Charles and Pat got pins-and-needles from keeping so still and they ran off to ride their hobby horses.

They were so glad that the robins had chosen to make a nest in their pillar-box. They looked forward to seeing the robin babies when the right time came.

12. Little Wife Goody

There was once a little boy named Ben who lived by the sea. When he looked out of his bedroom window, he could see a smooth, sandy beach with the waves breaking in curving ripples. When he lay awake in bed, early in the morning, he could hear the lap-lap of the water and the cries of the seagulls.

Ben had never played in a park, and the cottage where he lived had a very tiny garden. The beach was his playing place. He had only to open the front door, run across a rough, sandy track, down some stone steps, and he was on the sea shore. If his mother wanted him, she just called, 'Ben! Ben!' and he heard and ran home.

His favourite toys were his spade and pail, and his green shrimping net. Sometimes he caught a few shrimps. Sometimes he caught a crab. Sometimes he caught only seaweed. Whatever it was, he looked at it carefully, and then threw it back into the sea, where it belonged.

Ben had a big sister named Martha, with two long brown plaits hanging over her shoulders. When she was not at school, she often played with him and told him stories. There was a low stone wall between the sandy track and the beach, and Martha and Ben used to lean on the wall and look out to sea. Far away, over the sea, they could see another beach with golden sand.

'It is just like your beach, really,' said their mother. 'Children play on it just as you play here.' But Martha and Ben pretended it was quite different. They called it The Lucky Land, and made up stories about it.

'Everyone has strawberry jam for tea in The Lucky Land,' Ben would say.

'No one gets tangles in their hair,' added Martha, shaking her two long plaits, 'and they don't have to make their beds.'

'And boys don't need to wash. They just stay dirty.'

'And girls have lots of pockets – big ones – four in every dress.'

One morning, the postman came along the sandy path and knocked on the door of Ben's cottage, and Ben ran to open it.

'This is for you,' said the postman, giving him a small, square parcel.

'Thank you,' said Ben, jumping up and down with excitement. 'It is from granny. I know her nice curly B's. No one does such curly B's as granny.' Although Ben could not read yet, he knew how to write his own name.

He undid the string, took off the brown paper, and underneath was a piece of white paper. He took that off, and underneath was some soft tissue paper. Inside the soft tissue paper was a tiny wooden figure, like a tiny wooden doll. It was an old woman with a blue shawl over her head, and a yellow blouse, and a striped skirt. Her clothes were only painted on. She was shaped rather like an acorn, but flat at the bottom, so that she could stand. She was so small that she fitted inside Ben's hand.

'I shall call her Little Wife Goody,' said Ben, looking at her rosy cheeks and her smile. Then he noticed a crack round her middle, where her waist was. He held her tightly, gripped her head, and twisted it round. Yes, it

turned a little, and then a little more, and a little more, till she had come right in half. He held her top half in one hand and her bottom half in the other. She was hollow inside and in the hollow was a little red ball.

Ben took out the little red ball and looked at it carefully, but it was too tiny to unscrew.

'It must be Little Wife Goody's heart,' he said, and he put it back inside her and screwed her two halves together again.

Ben liked Little Wife Goody very much, from the

first moment he saw her. She was so bright and smiling and such a comfortable size for carrying about. He never went anywhere without her. Sometimes she was inside his hand, safe and warm. Sometimes she was inside his pocket. At meal times she sat on the table beside his plate. At night she slept under his pillow.

Martha liked Little Wife Goody as well. When Ben let her slip down the crack of the arm chair, down, down, where his fingers could not reach, Martha poked and prodded till she felt Little Wife Goody's head, and caught hold of it, and pulled her up to safety.

'We'll make some magic,' said Martha. 'Then she may not get lost again. Come with me and I'll show you how to do it.'

First they went into the little garden.

'Roll her three times in the soil,' said Martha, 'and then nothing on earth can hurt her.' So Ben rolled Little Wife Goody three times in the soil.

'Now dip her three times in water so nothing in the water can hurt her.' So Ben put some water in a bowl and dipped Little Wife Goody three times.

'Now wave her three times in the air so nothing in the air can hurt her.' So Ben waved Little Wife Goody three times in the air.

He felt very pleased that he had made magic. He

hoped dear Little Wife Goody would always be safe, on land, or water, or in the air.

Little Wife Goody had a very happy life with Ben. No wonder she smiled all the time. He made her gardens on the beach, with shells round the edge and seaweed for flowers. He made sand-castles with tunnels through them, and put her on the top. He dug holes so deep that the water rose and filled them like a lake, and he floated a boat on the lake, with her on board.

One day, when the tide was high and the waves covered the beach, Ben was leaning on the wall looking over the sea to The Lucky Land. The sun was shining and the sand was golden, it was so bright that he had to crinkle up his eyes. He held Little Wife Goody on the wall so she could look at The Lucky Land as well. The waves were breaking at the foot of the wall – splash! splash! splash! The spray was cold and wet on his face.

Suddenly, Ben never knew how, Little Wife Goody slipped off the wall and fell down, down, down, into the water. The tide had just turned, and a great wave curled over and flung her away from the wall. Her little blue head bobbed for a minute, and then another wave broke and carried her further away. And another. And another.

'Oh dear!' cried Ben. 'She's gone. She's drowned. Oh, what shall I do? Martha! Martha! Hurry – M-A-R-T-H-A!'

Martha came running out of the cottage and stood beside him. They both watched the little blue head bobbing up and down, up and down, among the waves.

'She won't drown,' said Martha. 'See how well she swims. Remember the magic you made to keep her safe in water.'

'But I made the magic with water from the tap, not salt water,' said Ben miserably.

'I'll get daddy's telescope and we'll look through that,' said Martha, running indoors.

By now, Little Wife Goody was only a speck. Ben tried to look through the telescope, but it was not much good. The sea was so big, and Little Wife Goody was so small. Tears kept coming into his eyes and making everything look blurred and misty.

Martha took the telescope and watched a little longer. 'She's still swimming. She's a wonderful swimmer. A seagull has just flown over her.'

Soon, even the tiny blue speck that was Little Wife Goody's head had floated out of sight. There were only the waves to watch, tossing the white foam like white horses tossing their manes.

Ben stayed by the wall till it was dinner time. Mother had poached him an egg in a nest of mashed potato but it was difficult to swallow. He did miss Little Wife Goody, standing by his plate, smiling. Afterwards, Martha read him a story and mother took him to the village in the bus but he did not feel much better. He wished he had Little Wife Goody in his hand instead of his bus ticket. She was such a smooth comfortable shape for holding. Just the right size.

When bed time came, Ben could not get to sleep. He turned his pillow over to find a cool place, and he heard the clock downstairs strike eight. He wondered where Little Wife Goody was sleeping. Was she still swimming in the water, bobbing up and down among the waves?

Just when he had decided that he never would get to sleep and he would have to stay awake till morning, Martha came in. She was wearing her dressing-gown, and her long plaits swung like two ropes as she sat on his bed and leaned over him.

'Ben,' she whispered, 'I've heard from Little Wife Goody. She's quite safe.'

Ben sat straight up. 'Where is she?'

'She has landed in The Lucky Land. It was a long journey over the sea, up and down among the waves, but at last, a wave washed her safely on to the shore.'

'How do you know?' asked Ben.

'A seagull brought me the news. When she found herself on the beach, she sat on a rock to get dry, and while she was resting and getting dry, dozens of little wooden

people, just like herself, came from holes in the rocks and under the seaweed. Big ones and small ones. Talking ones and quiet ones. Children and babies. They all said, "Welcome, Little Wife Goody. Welcome to The Lucky Land".'

'Is she happy away from me?'

'Well, she isn't exactly happy, because she likes you

best. She says she always will. But the little wooden people are very kind to her. She says, "Good night. Sleep tight".'

While Ben was thinking about Little Wife Goody and The Lucky Land, he fell fast asleep. Martha tiptoed away and put her bedroom slipper in the door to keep it from closing, so she could hear if Ben called. But Ben did not call. He slept till morning.

The next day Martha and Ben took a picnic to a cave in another part of the beach. They collected seaweed and made a seaweed garden, and Ben forgot about Little Wife Goody for quite a long time. But when they got home and he went to bed, he wished she was under his pillow where he could touch her. Martha came in to say good night.

'Any more news?' asked Ben.

'Yes. The Lucky Land people like Little Wife Goody so much that they want her to be their queen. They have made her a shell crown. She is very busy looking after people who are not well, and hushing babies who cry, and teaching the children to play "hunt the thimble" with a pebble.'

'Does she wish I was there with her?'

'Yes, she does. Always. She looks over the sea to your beach and wonders what you are doing.'

Every evening, Martha gave Ben news of Little Wife Goody. She was a kind queen. She taught the little wooden people to sing and make seaweed gardens. They had never heard of cereal for breakfast, or pancakes with lemon, so she had to do a lot of cooking.

One evening, Martha said, 'The seagull cannot come for a little while. He has to help his wife to build a nest. But Little Wife Goody says she is sending you a friend to keep you company. Look on the beach tomorrow at nine o'clock and you will find him.'

Next morning Ben could hardly wait till the clock had struck nine. He ran out of the door, over the sandy path, and down the steps to the beach. He ran here, there, everywhere, searching among the seaweed and the stones. Soon he saw a parcel with a label tied on. The label said: TO BEN FROM LITTLE WIFE GOODY. He opened the parcel and inside was a little wooden clown.

The clown was the same size as Little Wife Goody, like a big acorn, and he came in half round the middle just like her. And he had a red heart inside, too. He wore a pointed clown's hat, and had dabs of red on his cheeks and on his nose, like a real clown. And red pompoms on his hat and on his shirt. Of course, all these clothes were painted on.

As for his face, it was smiling, a great, wide, happy, ear-to-ear smile. Ben just had to smile back.

'I shall call my clown Smiling Sam,' he said, 'and I shall take him everywhere with me.'

So Smiling Sam went everywhere with Ben. He went on the beach. He sat on the table at meal times. He slept under Ben's pillow at night.

When Martha came to say good night, she asked Ben, 'What has Smiling Sam been doing today?' and Ben told her, 'He has been sailing in my boat,' or 'He has been building a sand-castle with six windows,' or 'He has been collecting oyster shells.'

When the tide is really high and the waves break against the sea wall, Ben puts Smiling Sam safely in his pocket. He looks across the water to the shore of The Lucky Land, and he wonders what Little Wife Goody is doing. But he cannot quite remember what Little Wife Goody looks like. So he brings Smiling Sam out of his pocket and looks at him instead. He is always smiling, from ear to ear. He even smiles when he is asleep, so he must have happy dreams.

13. The Cottage by the Sea

1

Once upon a time there were three children who lived in a little village by the sea. Their cottage had white-washed walls, a brown roof, and a curl of smoke coming from the chimney. The children were named Jenny, and Emma, and William. Jenny was the oldest. She was ten, Emma was eight, and little William was six.

When the children looked out of the window of their living-room, they could see the sandy beach curved like a new moon, and a small, stone jetty or pier stretching out like a long arm into the sea. The stones of the jetty were rough and uneven, but the children's bare feet were so tough and hard that they could run and jump on them as easily as on soft grass.

Here and there among the stones were heavy, iron rings where the fishermen could tie up their boats. Their father tied his boat to one of these rings. It was an old boat with patched sails but he was very proud of it.

The children's mother was usually very busy, cooking and washing and mending. Whenever the children went out to play, she always said, 'Don't go where you can't see the smoke from our chimney.' So they played on the beach or on the cliffs behind the cottage but never went so far that they could not see the curl of smoke. Then their mother knew they were safe.

One Saturday in summer, their mother said, 'You are getting big now, and sensible as well. You can go further away if you wish, along the cliff top. I will give you some lunch to take with you, but you must be home before the sun sets.'

The children promised not to stay out too late. They put their food in a satchel, and Jenny, because she was the oldest, slipped it over her shoulder.

'Good-bye, Mother!' they called, 'Good-bye! We'll be very careful and good.'

The three children followed the little winding cliff path, among the green leaves of the bracken and the prickly yellow gorse. They were so hardy that even William did not care when his bare legs became scratched with the prickles. On and on along the path they went, sometimes stopping to look over the edge of the cliff, down to the sea below. They saw lovely sandy beaches and great, black rocks bearded with green seaweed. A seagull flew right past their faces and they could see his pink feet tucked underneath him.

'I hope we aren't lost,' said Emma, who was not very brave. 'Shall we go back now?'

'Of course we're not lost,' said Jenny. 'There is only this one path and it will lead us straight home when we are tired.'

Suddenly little William stopped and called to the others to come and stand beside him. They ran to him and looked down, down, over the cliff's edge. There, on the beach below, was an old cottage. It was a tumble-down place, not fit for anyone to live in, with slates missing from the roof, and bracken and nettles growing as high as the windows. But it must have been a pretty little house once, so snug and sheltered against the cliff.

'Let's go and explore,' said Jenny. 'I see a path leading down the cliff. Take my hand William, and you'll be all right.' They went down the steep little path and soon reached the cottage.

First they walked around the outside. They did not say a word, the cottage looked so sad and lonely. The door had rotted away and there was no glass in the windows. It was very quiet, with only the waves lapping on the shore and a seagull crying overhead.

After a time they were used to the silence and the strangeness, and William went to the door and stepped inside the front room. The other two followed.

This room was draughty, and there were ferns and toadstools growing out of the floor. But there was another room beyond, and that was more comfortable.

'Look! Look!' cried William. 'Just look here!'

They crowded into the next room after him and saw, in the fireplace, the remains of a fire. Nearby was a pile of driftwood, neatly stacked. Against the wall was a bed of piled-up bracken leaves.

'Someone lives here,' whispered Emma. 'Someone sleeps here. I wonder whoever it could be!'

Jenny stooped and put her hand into the ashes in the fireplace. 'They are still warm,' she said. 'Someone must have cooked his breakfast here this morning.'

The children tried to imagine who could want to live in such a place. A tramp, perhaps. A gypsy. Someone very poor who had no money to pay for a proper bed.

They tiptoed out into the sunshine and ate their lunch sitting on a rock. Their mother had given them thick, thick slices of bread, chunks of cheese, three wedges of gingerbread, three rosy apples, and a bag of toffees.

'Shall we leave something in the little cottage for the person who sleeps there?' suggested Jenny. 'I can spare my apple. And a piece of toffee,' she added after a pause.

'So can I,' said Emma.

'I suppose I can, too,' said William, who wanted to eat his apple himself but did not like to seem greedy. So they put the three apples and the three pieces of toffee on the bracken bed.

Then Emma picked a bunch of sea pinks that were growing in the sand outside the cottage. She arranged them and put damp moss round the stalks to keep them fresh. William added a few bits of driftwood to the neat pile to help the person who lived in the cottage to make his fire. Then they scrambled up the steep path and turned back towards home. They reached their door just as the sun was setting, and their mother was buttering new scones for their tea.

During the next few days, the children often thought about the deserted cottage. If there was a strong wind, they wondered how the stranger who slept there kept warm. How the wind would whistle through the chinks in the walls and the holes in the roof! If the night was calm and mild, they were glad. The bracken bed would be quite comfortable on such a night.

The next Saturday was sunny and the children asked their mother to pack up another picnic for them. So she filled the satchel with good things to eat, and they set off along the cliff path. They had the whole day ahead of

them, hours and hours, but they could not help hurrying. Jenny strode on so quickly that Emma got out of breath, keeping up with her. As for William, he had to trot very fast on his short legs. But he did not mind. He was longing to see the little cottage again and to find out if the apples and the toffees were gone. If they were still there, he decided to eat his straight away, even if the toffee had gone soft and was sticking to the paper.

It did not seem long before they reached the steep cliff path, and went sliding and slithering down from the cliff top on to the beach. They ran to the door of the cottage, and then drew back. Suppose someone were inside? They did not want to burst in and disturb him. It was very quiet standing there, with the waves gently breaking, and the ivy flapping in the breeze.

'Is there anyone at home!' called Jenny softly. Her voice echoed queerly, but there was no answer, only a seagull crying.

'Let's go in,' whispered William. 'I'll go, if you'll come too.' He tiptoed into the first room and then through to the second room. Jenny and Emma were close behind him. Somehow, after one glance, they knew the room was quite deserted. The ashes had blown about the floor. There was no pile of driftwood. The fireplace was cold when they knelt down to feel it with their hands.

'He has gone away,' said Jenny.

'And our apples and toffees have gone, too,' added William. 'I expect he enjoyed them. He must have wondered who put them on his bed.'

'But he has left something else behind,' said Emma. 'Look! On this stone in the corner! And there's a piece of paper with writing on it.'

The writing was very smudged and thick, as if it had been done with the end of a burnt stick. It just said: THANK YOU.

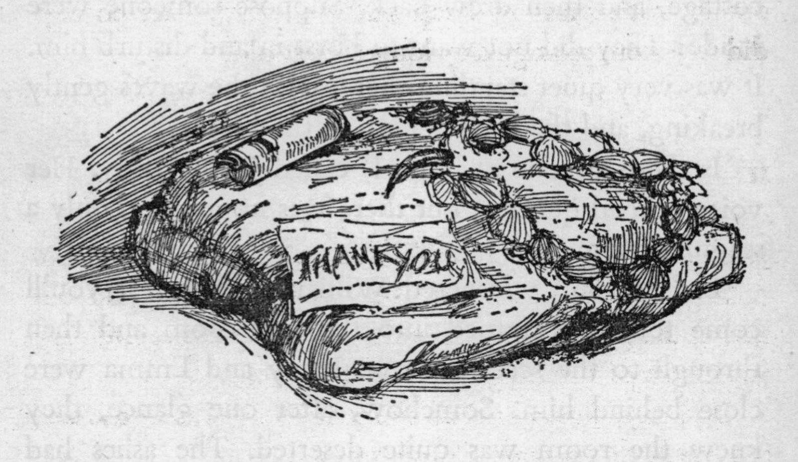

Beside the paper were three objects which made the children gasp with delight. There was a whistle carved from a piece of wood, a polished, black tooth of a shark, and a necklace of fan-shaped shells.

'One each!' said Emma. 'What a kind, clever man!' There was no arguing or quarrelling, because the presents just suited the children perfectly.

William reached for the whistle as Emma stretched out her hand for the shark's tooth. Jenny tied the necklace of shells round her neck.

They ate their picnic, every bit this time, and played round the cottage till it was time to go home. They mended some of the holes with stones, and packed the cracks with moss to keep out the wind. The cottage did not seem strange any longer. Just old.

II

Jenny, and Emma, and William often visited the old cottage on the beach, and played there. They did not forget the person who once slept in the cottage, and they took care of the presents he left behind.

One day, Jenny said to their mother, 'Do come and see our little cottage. Come today.'

'Yes, please come,' went on Emma.

'It isn't too far for you,' added William kindly. 'My legs hardly ache at all, now I know the way.'

'Very well,' said their mother. 'You go off now, and I'll come later, when I am ready. I will bring the picnic with me.'

The children rushed away. When they reached the cottage, they took off their jerseys, as they were hot, and hung them on a stick wedged beside the door. This made the cottage look like home.

'I'm going to make a surprise for Mother,' said Jenny.

'So am I,' said Emma. 'A really good one.'

'And so am I,' added William. 'I won't even tell you what it is going to be. Anyhow, I can't tell you. I don't know myself yet!'

Jenny found a flat slate that had fallen from the roof, and she propped it up on four stones to make a table. On the table she put round oyster shells for plates, and small, curly ones, like snail shells, for cups. She found a few blackberries for each plate, growing on the side of the cliff, and she put rosettes and ribbons of seaweed here and there to look pretty. Then she floated yellow gorse flowers in a big, deep shell in the middle of the table.

Emma wrote MOTHER in the sand with a stick, and then filled in the letters with pebbles.

Little William was busy with something very secret. 'Go away!' he shouted, if Jenny or Emma came near, 'Go away!'

Mother arrived at the right moment, when the surprises were ready. She called to them from the top of the cliff, and William scrambled up the path to take her hand, and help her down.

First mother looked at Jenny's surprise. 'I wish I was

small enough to sit at that dear little table,' she said. 'May I eat one of the blackberries?'

Then she admired her name written in pebbles. 'I did not know Emma could write so well. What a big, beautiful M!'

Now it was William's turn. 'Come with me,' he whispered. 'Come with me to my surprise.'

They all followed him. He had dug a deep hole in a bank of sand. 'That is my oven,' he explained. 'I'm a baker. Here are my buns.' He showed them four white stones on a slate. 'Now I am going to bake them in my hot oven.' He wrapped a handkerchief round his hand, as if the slate were too hot to hold, and pushed the buns into the oven.

'They're ready now,' he said after a pause. 'They're nicely done, I'm sure. What a lovely smell!'

He put his hand into the oven and fumbled about inside, making clinking noises. Then he pulled out the slate and there were four BROWN stones on it, instead of white.

'See, my buns are brown!' he cried, jumping up and down. 'My hot oven has cooked them. What do you think of that?'

'I think it is wonderful,' said mother. 'What a good baker you are! Not one is burnt!'

Then it was mother's turn to give the children a surprise. Beside sandwiches and apples for the picnic, she had brought three little biscuit men, one each. They had raisins for eyes and nose, a cherry for a mouth, and a row of raisin buttons for the jacket.

The children nibbled an arm or a leg first, whichever took their fancy, and then a bit of hat, till there was no biscuit man left.

After they had shown their mother the cottage, and played a little longer, it was time to go home. Jenny and Emma led the way, jumping over the prickly weeds. William, tired but happy, walked with mother, holding her hand, and sometimes blowing his whistle.

14. When I was Small as a Pin

Do you like to hear stories about yourself when you were very small? Charles liked to be told about himself when he slept in a crib and sat in a high chair and had gloves with no fingers like little woolly bags. But sometimes he liked to be told stories about himself that were only pretend ones, made-up ones. He liked to pretend he was once as small as a pin. And his mother pretended too.

One day, Charles said to his mother, 'Tell me a story about me, myself. Tell about when I was small as a pin.'

'Very well,' said his mother. 'Where shall I begin?'

'Begin about your handbag,' said Charles. 'I like that part.'

So his mother began. 'When you were small as a pin, you always liked to be with me. Perhaps you were afraid of getting lost or stepped on or falling through a crack in the floor. So when I went out shopping, I took you with me, in my handbag.'

'In your brown one with the long zipper?' asked Charles.

'Yes, in that very same one. You played with my money and my keys and I could hear you, jingling them inside. Sometimes, for a surprise, I put some special things inside for you, some coloured beads and a paper-clip. And you played with them.'

'What did you do with me when you were busy washing?'

'I gave you some water in a thimble and you splashed about in it while I washed the clothes.'

'What did you do with me when you were cooking?'

'I had to be very careful as you wanted to peep into everything and I was afraid you might fall into the milk or get smothered in the flour. Or perhaps scratch yourself on the nutmeg grater. So I used to lean a wooden spoon against the basin and you climbed up the handle and then slid down. And climbed up and slid down. And climbed up and slid down. You liked sliding so much.'

'I still do,' said Charles. 'And what did I do while you cleaned the house?'

'Oh, I used to carry you around in the pocket of my apron and in every room you had a favourite place. In the dining-room you sat on a little china horse and pretended he was real. In my bedroom you hid in my gloves and I had to hunt for you. And in the bathroom you sat on the shelf and squeezed the toothpaste tube.'

'Did I squeeze it hard?'

'Not very, because you were so small.'

'What did I do when you ate your dinner?'

'I put you right next to the salt shaker.'

'Tell about my bed.'

'You slept in a match-box filled with cotton wool, on

the table by my bed. Once you ate a whole box of cherry cough drops that I had there.'

'Did they give me a pain?'

'Yes, they did. You cried.'

'How did I cry?'

'Ee – ee – ee – ee.'

'How did you make me happy again?'

'I showed you yourself in a mirror and you looked so funny with your little pin face screwed up and your little pin mouth saying 'ee – ee – ee' that you began to laugh.'

'It must have been very comfortable,' said Charles, 'to be so small and always to be with you.'

'But it's much nicer now,' said his mother. 'We can talk now and play together and I'm not afraid of losing you. You couldn't slip between the floor-boards now.'

'Or fall into the milk jug.'

'Or get stepped on.'

'And I'll never, never be lost,' said Charles. 'If I even *felt* lost for a minute I could always say my name and where I lived. Then someone would take me home.'

'So you could. Will you say them to me?'

'I'm Charles Cox and I live at 17 Hazel Road, Westbridge.'

That was a useful thing to know, wasn't it? Do you know your name and address like Charles?

15. The Robber

One morning, Hedgehog was scampering round the garden, his bristles shining in the sun, when he met his best friend Tortoise. Tortoise was often very lively at this hour, walking briskly along, his eyes bright and his flat head turning from side to side. But, today, he was sitting quite still, in one spot.

'You look very sad,' remarked Hedgehog.

'It's unfair!' muttered Tortoise, his head half hidden in the folds of his neck. 'It's a shame! It's a disgrace!'

'What is unfair?' asked Hedgehog.

'Food is unfair. Or rather *my* food is. I shall soon starve to death. When they find my dead body under the rhubarb leaves, they'll be sorry!'

'What do you mean? Do, please, explain,' Hedgehog wrinkled his little brown face into a frown. What he could see of Tortoise looked quite ordinary. Four stout, short legs. Tail as usual. Face as plump as ever, in spite of cross expression. But, of course, most of Tortoise was hidden under his hard shell. Perhaps he was shrinking under there, shrinking slowly, fading away out of sight.

'Everyone else has as much food as he or she can eat, and the right kind, too,' went on Tortoise. 'Owl catches as many mice as he can swallow. Dandy the dog is always burying bones he cannot finish. Winko the kitten has milk on his whiskers whenever I see him. And what did *you* find to eat last night for supper? Tell me that!'

'I don't remember exactly. A dozen or so worms, slugs and beetles, a snail or two, a few odds and ends by way of pudding, a couple of frogs, I believe.'

'A square meal! A positive feast! And where is *my* square meal? Where is *my* feast? Tell me that!'

Hedgehog shook his head. He did not know. Tortoise went on. 'Under wire netting, that's where it is. Under wire netting, safely fixed by the gardener to keep me out.'

'Yes. I saw him putting the lettuce bed into a kind of cage of wire netting. But this garden is full of things for you to eat. You are always chewing dandelions and yellow pansies and tender shoots.'

'Those are only extras. Mere titbits. Lettuce is my proper food. Crisp, young lettuce. Young, green, curly, crumpled little hearts that melt in the mouth.'

Hedgehog felt very sorry for his friend. He would

gladly have brought him a few juicy worms or a fat slug but Tortoise ate only green things.

'Let's ask Owl,' he suggested cheerfully. 'Owl will know what to do. He is so wise. Come along, now. We may just catch him before he goes to sleep after his night's hunting.'

They scurried off, Hedgehog running ahead and Tortoise following at a fine speed, considering he was about to die of starvation.

Owl had just tidied his hole in the hollow oak for the day, and preened his feathers. He was feeling drowsy, but he listened to Tortoise's sad tale without actually falling asleep in the middle.

'Grow lettuce yourself,' he advised, yawning and nodding.

'Where can I get the seed?'

'Shelf in the tool-shed.'

'Where shall I plant them?'

'Anywhere.'

'But I can't read what it says on the seed packets.'

This time there was no answer, only a snore. Owl was asleep.

Tortoise and Hedgehog hurried to the tool-shed. They could not reach the high shelf themselves where the seeds were kept, but young Twig Squirrel climbed

up and brought them down. Luckily there was a picture of each plant on the outside of the packet, so there was no need to worry over the writing.

Tortoise was tempted to grow radishes when he saw the round, rosy ones in the picture. How good they would be to crunch, but perhaps a little hard. He turned to the next packet.

This showed neat rows of peas, each pod ready to burst open. But the pods were rather high and he was a short kind of animal. He pondered over beans. Cabbages. Carrots. Then he gazed at gay pictures of pinks and

cornflowers. But when Twig Squirrel handed him a packet of lettuce seeds, he forgot everything else. The picture showed an enormous lettuce. A giant lettuce. Almost all heart and no outside to speak of.

Twig put the other packets back on the shelf and Tortoise went off with the lettuce packet in his mouth. He planned to meet Twig and Hedgehog that evening and make a seed bed. He spent the day looking at the packet and planning where he would take his first bite – right in the very middle of the curly heart!

When evening came, and the gardener had gone home, and Teddy and Susan, who played in the garden, were in bed, Tortoise met his friends among the raspberries. Dandy and Winko came as well, and several mice and squirrels.

'We must choose a very secret place for my seed bed,' said Tortoise, 'where we shall not be disturbed.'

'What about the patch by the pond?'

'That's far too open. Everyone will see us.'

'Or the bit near the holly bush?'

'That's too shadowy. Nothing will grow.'

Almost every inch of the garden was suggested in turn and someone found something wrong with it.

'Let me flip a nutshell into the air,' said Twig Squirrel, 'while you all cross your paws for luck. Where it falls we will have the seed bed.'

'We can try,' agreed Tortoise, doubtfully, 'but I can't cross my paws. They aren't arranged that way.'

Twig quickly found an old nutshell and gave it a sharp flick. Up in the air it went – over the lilac – and down in a sheltered corner between the summer-house and the hedge. Everyone gave a sigh of relief, and paws were uncrossed. They set to work at once.

The seed bed, when finished, would have pleased a real gardener. So many claws and paws had scratched and raked it over that the soil was as fine and soft as sand. Then Tortoise, trembling with excitement, bit off the corner of the packet, and slowly crept up and down, letting the seed fall out in a thin line. Hedgehog followed, covering the seed lightly, while Dandy brought a can of water from the pond in his mouth and watered the bed well.

Tired but happy, Tortoise crept away to his bedroom under the rhubarb leaves, and dreamed of giant lettuces, rows and rows of them, all his own.

Tortoise spent most of his time in his new garden, making sure that no robber bird stole a single seed. In a week, the first green shoots appeared. Here Owl came in useful. He had once read a gardening book and remembered some of the hints. He gave good advice to Tortoise and his helpers.

'Water well,' he said, and they watered well.

'Thin out the seedlings,' and they thinned out the seedlings.

'Hoe! Transplant! Weed! Thin again!' As these wise words came from the hollow oak, they were acted on at once. The little garden would have taken first prize in a competition. Not a weed. Not a stone. Not a drooping plant. Only fine, young lettuce, evenly spaced out.

They were not, it is true, *quite* as large and juicy as the

ones in the picture on the packet but each grew a tight little heart, and, at last, Tortoise said that the very next day he intended to eat one for breakfast.

Early in the morning, Tortoise went to his garden to choose the first lettuce. The hedge smelled sweet with the dew still on it, and the sun shone warmly. His cry of horror, when he saw what had happened during the night, brought Hedgehog and Twig and the others quickly to his side. Then their cries were joined with his. Every lettuce had a nibble taken out of its heart. Not one had escaped. Some robber had tasted each in turn.

Tortoise almost wept with rage and despair. Dandy howled. Winko mewed. Hedgehog growled. The squirrels wrung their paws and the mice squeaked.

'It's only a very tiny nibble,' said Dandy at last. 'The lettuces aren't exactly spoiled.'

'But they *are* spoiled,' raged Tortoise. 'Quite, quite spoiled. Do you think I am going to eat other people's leavings? Not I! I shall keep watch tonight, and if the robber comes again, I'll give him what he deserves.'

'I'll watch with you,' offered several animals, but Tortoise refused their help.

'No, thank you. I shall keep watch alone. I can deal with him single-handed. I'll bite his nose! I'll scratch out his eyes! I'll tear his ears off! I'll make his fur fly!'

As Tortoise was the most gentle and timid of creatures, these threats sounded specially horrible.

'I'll jag him into a jig-saw!' went on Tortoise. 'I'll rip him into ribbons!' The others felt almost sorry for the robber, wicked though he was. Did he really deserve to have all these terrible things done to him?

That night, Tortoise hid under the hedge, and dozed lightly till the first cock crowed. There were all the usual early morning sounds. Birds stirring in their nests. Drowsy chirpings. A distant train. But when would that other sound begin? Stealthy feet, perhaps creeping, perhaps scampering. His nose sniffed the air for a strange smell.

Suddenly he lifted his head. The robber was coming, nearer, and nearer. There was a scratching of dry soil as someone pressed through the hedge. In a few seconds Tortoise would be able to see him, face to face.

The robber walked quite openly into view, looking about boldly, not trying to hide. Why did not Tortoise attack him? Bite him and scratch him? Jag him into a jig-saw? Make his fur fly?

To begin with, there was no fur to fly. The robber was mostly shell and scaly skin. No wonder Tortoise opened his eyes very wide with surprise when he saw, in front of him, an elegant and charming lady tortoise. He came from his hiding place, unable to say a word.

'Good morning, Sir,' said the lady tortoise. 'Are you the owner of this delighful lettuce garden? I have never seen a more beautiful one, not in all my travels, and I may say that I have lived in many strange places.'

'Yes, it's mine,' answered Tortoise gruffly. 'It's mine all right.'

'How very kind of you to allow me to feast off your

home-grown salad. Remarkably kind! Especially as we have not been introduced. My name is Princess Dido and I come from Greece.'

'They just call me Tortoise.'

'A plain, noble name. Will you let me pay for what I have already eaten? A bunch of dandelions, perhaps, or a few young radishes?'

'Certainly not,' protested Tortoise. 'Eat all you want, when you want. I feel ready for breakfast myself. Will you join me as my guest?'

Princess Dido was willing and the pair of them ate together, a nibble here and there, talking between mouthfuls.

'I came from the land of Greece in a barrel,' said Princess Dido, 'with dozens and dozens of my relations. Some men grabbed us from the peaceful rocks, where we were basking in the sun, and packed us in so tightly that we could hardly breathe. Then they nailed the lid on the barrel. Oh, how we longed for water and fresh food! Many of us died. The little ones, no bigger than crab-apples, died first. But I lived through the long voyage, perhaps because I was pressed against a crack in the side of the barrel. I could get a taste of sea air.

'I was taken to a shop, and the people who bought me were kind. But I missed my freedom. I was used to rocks, and the smell of wild thyme, and the company of my brothers and sisters. They bored a hole in my shell, threaded a string through, and tied me to a post, so I was a prisoner. But I bit through the string and escaped, and, after a long and weary journey, I found my way to your quiet garden.'

Tortoise was shocked to see the hole in the Princess's shell. What could be worse than not being able to go where one wanted? Tortoise described the garden, and the animals and birds who lived there. He suggested that the Princess should pay him a long visit, and meet all his friends. She accepted the invitation, gladly.

In the meantime, Hedgehog, and Twig Squirrel, and the others had tiptoed near to see what was happening. They expected to find a horrid scene. Blood splashed everywhere. Fur flying. Probably a dead body among the lettuce. All they saw, however, was Tortoise and a small, charming companion, very like himself but lighter in colour, strolling up and down, eating and chatting.

Owl looked down upon them from the roof of the summer-house. He was never surprised at anything, and only remarked. 'Two's company. Three's none,' and flew off to his oak tree. He had had a good night's hunting, and wanted to go to sleep.

The other animals stole away as Tortoise offered Princess Dido a juicy lettuce heart, saying in a happy voice, 'I used to feel lonely before you came. Now I shall have a companion. There are so many things I want to tell you that only another tortoise could understand.'

'Of course,' answered the Princess, taking the lettuce heart with a smile. 'I, too, have much to tell. Now when I lived in Greece . . .'

16. Granny-by-the-Sea

Charles liked staying by the sea with granny. He liked everything there, the house, the garden, granny's ginger cat, and the brown sugar he was given to sprinkle over his porridge in the morning. But of course the best thing of all was the sea itself. He wanted to spend every minute on the beach and he thought that shopping or going for a walk was a waste of time.

The first time Charles saw the sea he was only two years old and he ran right into the water, before anyone could catch him, and soaked his new brown sandals and his shorts and half his blouse as well! Now he was four, he was too sensible to get wet with all his clothes on. He waited till he was wearing his bathing suit, or at least till he had taken off his shoes and socks.

Granny knew just how much Charles liked being on the beach. When he arrived, with his luggage, and his Useful Bag slung over one shoulder, she never bothered about unpacking and putting things in drawers straight away. She gave him a glass of milk and then they both put on their sun hats and went down the steep cliff path to the beach. Granny came slowly behind holding on to the wooden railing at the side, but Charles ran like the wind. When he got to the bottom of the path there were three steps and he took a great, big, flying jump down these and landed in the soft sand which filled his shoes. But this did not matter as he just sat down plomp and took off his shoes and socks and left them lying there and ran on towards the water's edge. Granny, coming along behind, picked up the shoes and socks and stuffed them in the beach bag with the towel and the spare jersey and the other things she kept there.

The sea was always a little colder than Charles expected. He said 'O – oh! O – oh!' with surprise when the cold, clear waves washed over his feet and ankles. 'O – oh! O – oh!'

The sand by the edge of the sea was damp and dark

and firm while the sand higher up the beach, where granny sat, was dry and pale and powdery. There were two games Charles liked to play with sand, one game with the damp sand and one with the dry. I will tell you what he did with the damp sand first.

He got his spade and bucket from granny, filled his bucket full of sand, well pressed down, and he turned the bucket upside down. He patted the bottom of it with his spade, like this – tap! tap! tap! Then, very carefully, he lifted up the bucket and there stood a perfect sand pie, just the size of the bucket. Charles made one pie for granny and one for mother and one for daddy and one for his other granny and one for himself. That was five. They stood in a row and he put a special thing on each to make it pretty. One had a cockle shell. One had a white stone. One had some green seaweed. One had a pink shell. His own was very grand with a paper flag on a stick. Granny made the flag out of an envelope and Charles put it on the stick.

Now I will tell you about the other game Charles played with the dry, powdery sand. He scooped a hollow in the sand with his hands and lay down in it. 'Please bury me,' he said to granny, and if she was not too busy knitting or writing letters she always did.

First she buried his legs. His toes disappeared and his feet and his knees. Then his shorts disappeared and his chest and his arms and his neck. There was only his head peeping out.

'Bury my face, please bury my face,' begged Charles. But granny always said: 'No dear, not your face. You would get sand in your eyes and that would hurt. And sand in your nose and that would tickle. We'll just leave your face showing.'

Charles had to keep as still as a stone. If he moved the least, tiniest bit a toe would poke through the sand or a knee or a finger. He could not turn his head, so all he could see was some blue sky and a white cloud sailing across.

'It's time to go now,' said granny.

'But I can't move,' said Charles. 'I can't move at all. I'll never be able to move again.'

'I'm sorry to hear that,' said granny, not at all worried because she knew Charles was pretending.

'I'll have to stay here all night,' went on Charles. 'And all tomorrow. And the next day and the next.'

'What will you do when the tide comes up and washes over you?' asked granny.

'Jump up like a jack-in-the-box!' shouted Charles, leaping up in the air and scattering sand everywhere.

'Gracious me!' said granny. 'You gave me a terrible fright!' and she fanned herself with her knitting pattern. Charles gave her a hug and then she wasn't frightened any more and they went up the beach together, up the three steps and up the steep cliff path towards home. Charles held granny's hand all the way because he was tired and it was nearly his bedtime.

About the Author

Ruth Ainsworth has twin sons and one a year younger. When they lived in a very remote village before they went to school she used to tell them endless stories on walks and they told her wonderful ones too. The idea of Charles's Useful Bag came from one of the boys who carried a black shoe-bag around and almost any missing object could be found in it. Once, when he was three, he had 27 small things in his trouser pockets, and 19 in his coat pockets.

Ruth Ainsworth now lives in a village in the Tyne valley and likes reading and walking and seeing her grand-children and friends.

LUCKY DIP, her first collection of stories, is also available in a Young Puffin edition.

There are now nearly 100 Young Puffins to choose from, and some of them are described on the following pages

A Golden Land

ed. James Reeves

A wonderfully rich miscellany of stories, poems and rhymes, old and new, long and short, specially chosen by the poet and editor James Reeves to make storytime a real pleasure for both mother and child.

The Invisible Womble and Other Stories

Elisabeth Beresford

These five stories are retellings of some of the television adventures and reveal the Wombles at their funniest and best. This book will certainly ensure their place in the family long after they have left the studios and bolted the door of their burrow behind them.

The Bears on Hemlock Mountain

Alice Dalgliesh

'OF COURSE THERE ARE NO BEARS ON HEMLOCK MOUNTAIN,' said Jonathan to himself as he walked over the hill, but he was still afraid there might be!

Umbrella Thursday *and* A Helping Hand

Janet McNeill

Good deeds sometimes have funny results, as the two little girls in these stories discover.

Fattypuffs and Thinifers

André Maurois

Edmund loved food and was plump, but his brother Terry was very thin, and when they took a moving staircase to the Country Under the Earth, they found themselves split up and in the midst of the dispute between the Fattypuffs and the Thinifers.

My Naughty Little Sister
My Naughty Little Sister's Friends
When My Naughty Little Sister Was Good

Dorothy Edwards

These now famous stories were originally told by a mother to her own children. Ideal for reading aloud. For ages 4 to 8.

Five Dolls in a House

Helen Clare

A little girl called Elizabeth finds a way of making herself small and visits her dolls in their own house. Girls.

Flat Stanley

Jeff Brown and Tomi Ungerer

Stanley Lambchop was an ordinary boy, except for one thing: he was four feet tall, about a foot wide, and only half an inch thick!

Emily's Voyage

Emma Smith

Emily Guinea-Pig leaves her cosy home to go on her first sea voyage – only to be shipwrecked on a tropical island with the crew of frightened rabbits and their lackadaisical captain.

Clever Polly and the Stupid Wolf
Polly and the Wolf Again

Catherine Storr

Clever Polly manages to think of lots of good ideas to stop the stupid wolf from eating her.

Some Young Puffin Originals

Bad Boys

ed. Eileen Colwell

Twelve splendid stories about naughty boys, by favourite authors like Helen Cresswell, Charlotte Hough, Barbara Softly and Ursula Moray Williams.

Duggie and Digger and His Friends

Michael Prescott

As well as Duggie the Digger, there are tales about Horace the Helicopter, Bertram the Bus and Vernon the Vacuum Cleaner. It will please little boys who are interested in mechanical things.

Tales from the End Cottage
More Tales from the End Cottage

Eileen Bell

Two tabby cats and a peke live with Mrs Apple in a Northamptonshire cottage. They quarrel, have adventures and entertain dangerous strangers. A new author with a special talent for writing about animals. For reading aloud to 5 and over, private reading 7 plus.

Tales of Olga da Polga
Olga Meets Her Match

Michael Bond

Michael Bond's latest heroine is an enchantingly independent guinea-pig with a zest for adventure.

Something to Do

Septima

This Young Puffin Original gives suggestions for games to play and things to make and do each month, from January to December. It is designed to help mothers with young children at home.

Something to Make

Felicia Law

A varied and practical collection of things for children to make from odds and ends around the house, with very little extra outlay, by an experienced teacher of art and handicrafts. For children of 6 up.

This Little Puffin . . .

compiled by Elizabeth Matterson

A treasury of nursery games, finger plays and action songs, collected with the aid of nursery school teachers all over the British Isles. For parents of under-fives.

The Young Puffin Book of Verse

Barbara Ireson

A deluge of poems about such fascinating subjects as birds and balloons, mice and moonshine, farmers and frogs, pigeons and pirates, especially chosen to please young people of 4 to 8.

Puffin Book of Nursery Rhymes

Peter and Iona Opie

The first comprehensive collection of nursery rhymes to be produced as a paperback, prepared for Puffins by the leading authorities on children's lore, and exquisitely illustrated by Pauline Baynes.

Ponder and William
Ponder and William on Holiday

Barbara Softly

Ponder the panda looks after William's pyjamas and is a wonderful companion in these all-the-year-round adventures.